The Chu

GO SHOPPING

Story by Elizabeth Laird
Pictures by Carolyn Scrace

The Chunky Bears are going shopping.

Pa wants a watch strap.
Roly needs some shoes.
Poly wants a sweater.
And Oswald has run out of talcum powder.

There's a new clothes' shop in the high street.
"Perhaps we'll find my sweater in here,"
says Poly.

There are big sweaters and small sweaters, red sweaters and blue sweaters, and sweaters with pictures all over them.
But none of them are right for Poly.

The next shop along is a shoe shop.
"Do you think we'll find my shoes in
here?" says Roly.

There are school shoes and party shoes
snow boots and football boots,
and trainers with multi-coloured laces.
But none of them are right for Roly.

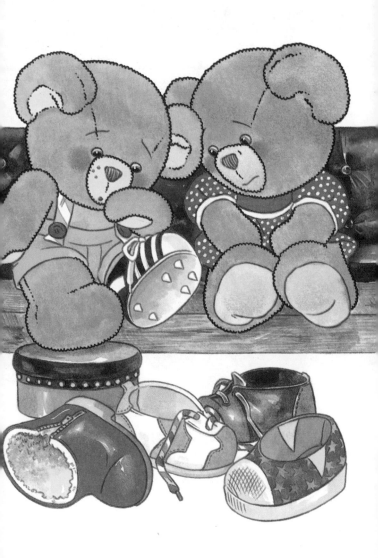

Not far away is the jewellers.
"We'll try and get my watchstrap
in here," says Pa.

There are gold straps and silver straps,
leather straps and plastic straps,
and straps that stretch when you
pull them.
But none of them was right for Pa.

"Oh dear," says Ma.
"We're not doing very well today."

"Here's the chemist," says Pa.
"Perhaps they'll have some talcum
powder for Oswald."

There's pink powder and white powder,
ladies' powder and babies' powder,
and powder in fancy packets.
And one of them is just right for Oswald.

The Chunky Bears go down to the
market. They have a good look round.

"They've got a bit of everything
here," says Ma.

"Pa! Pa!" says Roly.
"I can see just the shoes I want!"

He tries them on.
They look good, and they fit too.
"We'll take them," says Pa.

"Ma! Ma!" says Poly.
"There's just the sweater for me!"

She tries it on.
It's the right colour and the right size.
"We'll take it," says Ma.

"Well, Well," says Pa.
"Here's just the watchstrap I need!"

He picks it up. It looks hardwearing
and it's not expensive.
"I'll take it," says Pa.

The Chunky Bears go home.
Everyone's got something new.
All except Ma.

"Just a minute," says Pa.
He pulls something out of his pocket.

It's a scarf.
Ma tries it on. It suits her beautifully,
and it's warm, too.
"I think it's lovely," she says.